Thanks to Gees-Ineke Smit and Martijn Pronk for their valuable advice.

Also available as app: *Monkey & Mole* go to the seaside and *Monkey & Mole* at the RIJKSMUSEUM

Copyright © Text & illustrations 2013 Gitte Spee
Copyright © 2013 The House of Books, Vianen/Antwerpen

Design of cover & interior: steef liefting

ISBN 978 90 443 3910 9
NUR 272
D/2013/8899/50

www.gittespee.nl
www.rijksmuseum.nl
www.thehouseofbooks.com

monkey & mole
at the RIJKS
MUSEUM

gitte spee

the house of books

'Wow! This place is beautiful! It looks like a palace!' thinks Mole.

Mole wanted to dig a tunnel to the tree where his best friend Monkey lives.

But accidentally he ended up in a big building.

'Monkey has got to see this!' thinks Mole. And he runs back down the tunnel to look for Monkey.

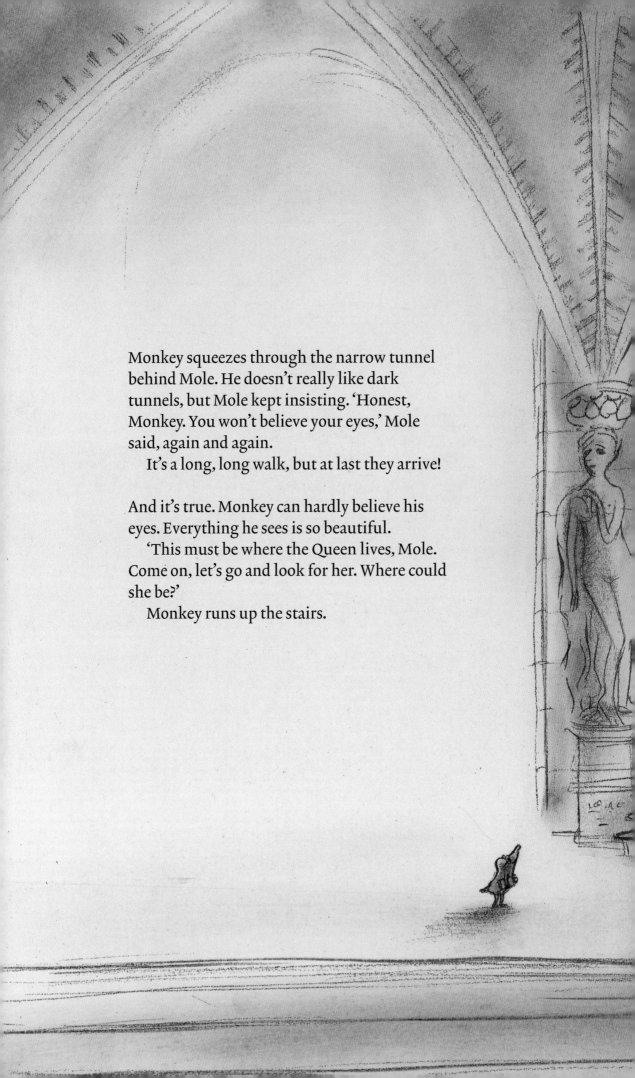

Monkey squeezes through the narrow tunnel
behind Mole. He doesn't really like dark
tunnels, but Mole kept insisting. 'Honest,
Monkey. You won't believe your eyes,' Mole
said, again and again.

It's a long, long walk, but at last they arrive!

And it's true. Monkey can hardly believe his
eyes. Everything he sees is so beautiful.

'This must be where the Queen lives, Mole.
Come on, let's go and look for her. Where could
she be?'

Monkey runs up the stairs.

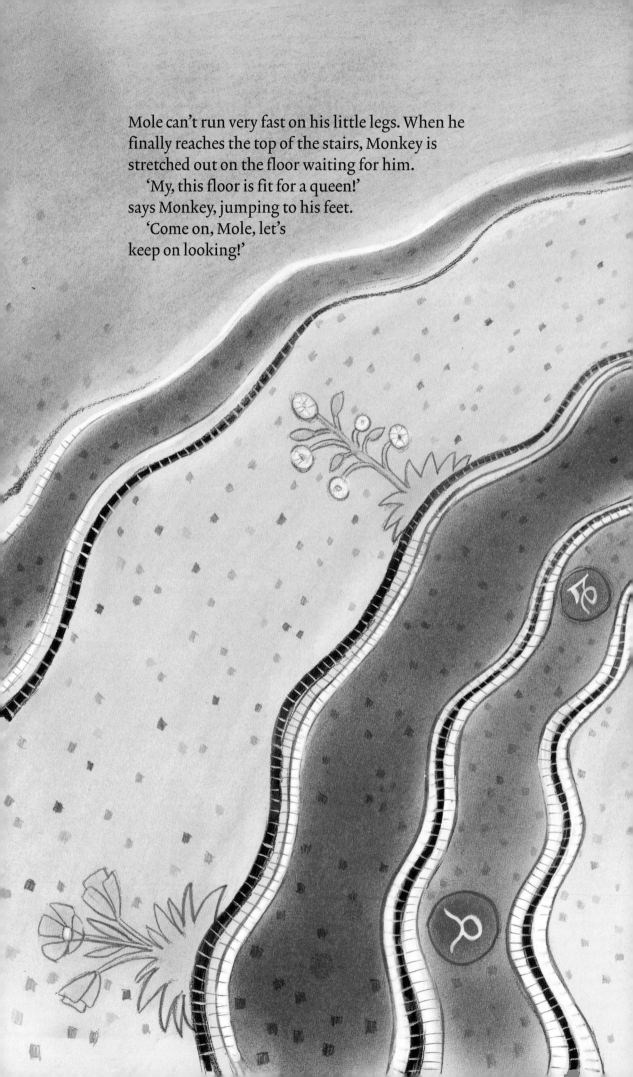

Mole can't run very fast on his little legs. When he finally reaches the top of the stairs, Monkey is stretched out on the floor waiting for him.

'My, this floor is fit for a queen!' says Monkey, jumping to his feet.

'Come on, Mole, let's keep on looking!'

'Look,' shouts Monkey, 'there's a big crowd of people over there.

I bet that's where the Queen is, Mole. She has a little dog with her.

Can you see it?'

Mole can hardly keep up with Monkey.

When they get closer, Monkey says in a worried
voice: 'Aw, the little dog looks sad.'

'No, he doesn't,' says Mole. 'He's just been startled by
the drum. Anyway, it's only a painting. It's all just paint.'
'You're right! Let's go on,' says Monkey.

Monkey and Mole wander through hallways and rooms. Mole is starting to get a little tired from all that walking.

But then he sees a house, a house in a cabinet.

'Monkey,' says Mole, 'why don't you keep on looking? I'll sit here quietly for a while and read my book.'

He climbs into the cabinet.

'What's going on?' a loud voice booms suddenly.

'The museum is closed. And animals aren't allowed in here!'

Monkey looks round in a fright and sees an angry man standing there.

'Come on, Mole. Let's get out of here!'

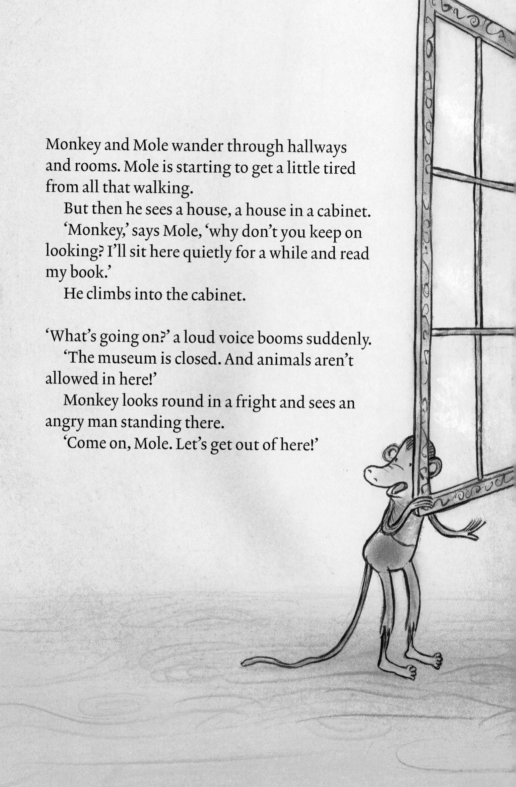

'Watch out, Monkey! He's right behind us!'
shouts Mole.

  Ouch! Monkey bumps into a tower and
nearly knocks it over. He catches it just in time.

'Quick! In here! Through the white door...' they
hear someone whisper.

They run through the doorway and see a little angel looking back at them.

'Sshh!' says the angel. 'Hide behind the white door until the security guard has gone.'

Monkey and Mole stand there, as quiet as mice.

They hear the guard's heavy footsteps pass by.

'You can come out now. The coast is clear,' says the angel.

'Thank you,' whisper Monkey and Mole and they sneak back into the hallway.

'That must be a guardian angel, Monkey,' says Mole.

Monkey and Mole wander on through endless hallways.
Now and then, they hear footsteps in the distance.
Suddenly the footsteps seem to get closer.
'Quick! Up these stairs, Monkey!'
In the room at the top of the stairs, they discover an
aeroplane.

'Hurray! We can make our getaway!' shouts
Monkey.
　'But how do we fly away, Monkey? The plane
can't fit through the window!'
　'Isn't that weird, Mole? We'll just have to keep
moving!'

Monkey and Mole keep on running. But the footsteps keep getting closer and closer. Monkey jumps into a big vase and Mole hides behind it.

'What's going on here? My precious vase is moving!' says a voice.

But this time it's a different voice, one that doesn't sound very angry.

Monkey feels brave enough to pop his head out.

'Ah, Mr Director sir, you've found them!' calls the guard.

'I'll throw them out at once. A museum is no place for animals.

Especially monkeys!'

'Don't worry, my good fellow. You don't have to throw them out,' says the director in a friendly voice. 'Besides, there are lots of animals in the museum.

Monkeys too! You two come with me and I'll show you.'

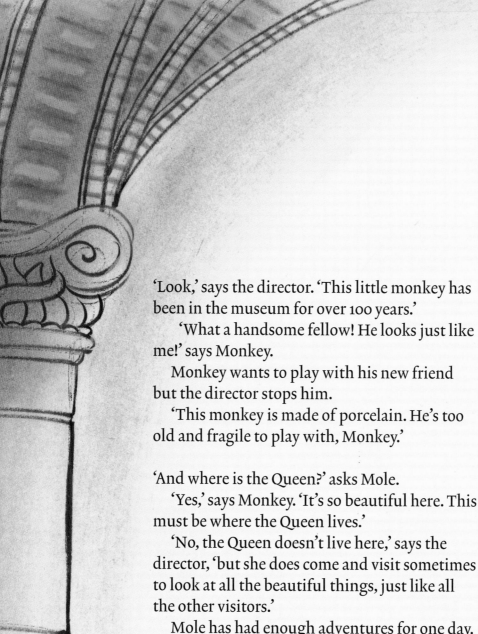

'Look,' says the director. 'This little monkey has been in the museum for over 100 years.'

'What a handsome fellow! He looks just like me!' says Monkey.

Monkey wants to play with his new friend but the director stops him.

'This monkey is made of porcelain. He's too old and fragile to play with, Monkey.'

'And where is the Queen?' asks Mole.

'Yes,' says Monkey. 'It's so beautiful here. This must be where the Queen lives.'

'No, the Queen doesn't live here,' says the director, 'but she does come and visit sometimes to look at all the beautiful things, just like all the other visitors.'

Mole has had enough adventures for one day. He misses the peace and quiet of his cosy little home.

'Shall we go, Monkey?'

'Will you come and see us again?' asks the director.

'Of course we will!' says Monkey. 'We want to visit all the animals that live here.'

And the two friends hop into Mole's tunnel and head back to the safety of the forest they know and love so well.

The End

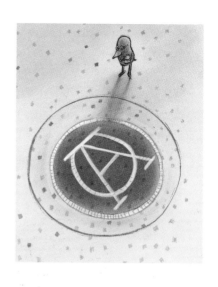

When Monkey and Mole get back to the forest, Mole can't wait to look at his books. He wants to find out about everything they saw at the museum. Let's see what he's found!

3 De *Nachtwacht* (The *Night Watch*) is the most famous painting in the Netherlands. It was painted by Rembrandt in 1642.

4 Petronella Oortman's dolls' house cost as much money as a real Amsterdam canal house when it was made in 1686.

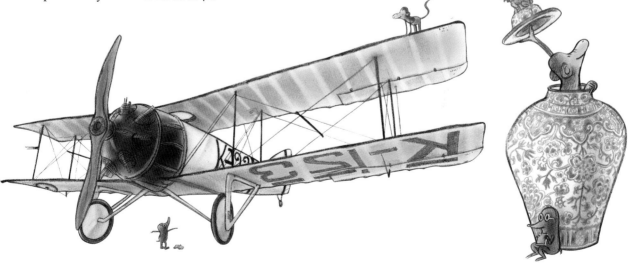

7 This fighter plane, the FK-23 Bantam, was designed in 1917 by Frits Koolhoven.

8 These big vases are Chinese. They were made in the Kangxi period (1661-1722). There is a gilded lion on each lid.